## About the Author

Colleen A. J. Smith is an artist and writer whose work has been exhibited in galleries throughout North America, Europe and the United Kingdom. Born and raised in Western Canada, Colleen received a double honors degree in Art History and Classical Studies from the University of Saskatchewan, before receiving her MFA in Drawing and Creative Research from the University of Calgary. Her work illuminates slivers of the beautiful, the banal, and our sense of belonging in-between. She currently lives and creates in the radiant city of Saskatoon, Saskatchewan. The Black Oasis is her first book.

# The Black Oasis

Colleen A. J. Smith

# The Black Oasis

Olympia Publishers
*London*

www.olympiapublishers.com
OLYMPIA PAPERBACK EDITION

Copyright © Colleen A. J. Smith 2024

The right of Colleen A. J. Smith to be identified as author of this work has been asserted in accordance with sections 77 and 78 of the Copyright, Designs and Patents Act 1988.

**All Rights Reserved**

No reproduction, copy or transmission of this publication may be made without written permission.
No paragraph of this publication may be reproduced, copied or transmitted save with the written permission of the publisher, or in accordance with the provisions of the Copyright Act 1956 (as amended).

Any person who commits any unauthorised act in relation to this publication may be liable to criminal prosecution and civil claims for damage.

A CIP catalogue record for this title is available from the British Library.

ISBN: 978-1-80439-471-7

This is a work of fiction.
Names, characters, places and incidents originate from the writer's imagination. Any resemblance to actual persons, living or dead, is purely coincidental.

First Published in 2024

Olympia Publishers
Tallis House
2 Tallis Street
London
EC4Y 0AB

Printed in Great Britain

# Dedication

For my mother, Ann. With all my heart. Thank you for being my Tabitha.

## Acknowledgments

For my brother, Jesse, my redwood tree. For my Auntie Viv, my tracks in the snow. For my Auntie Wendy, my river reflection. For all of my beautiful friends - truly bright beams of spirit who have loved me unconditionally since the moment I hurtled myself into their sparkling spheres of existence. For those I have loved like glowing embers in the rainfall. For Jaspreet, my sunrise of inspiration which has still not set. I am in love with and inspired by your spirit still. Gratias Ago Tibi.

## September 2022

I don't want my car to start dictating my time. Not when it dictates everything else about my existence. I can't let it. The concept of free time is all that I have left. And I have lots of it.

But I can't help it. If I don't use my car, I lose track of the days and nights. And if I lose track of time, then I lose track of myself. So, I keep doing it - punching holes in the leather of the car seat with a tiny screwdriver that I keep clipped to my keychain. It used to tighten the lens of my sunglasses. Now I use it for keeping time in the car. It's the key that winds my world.

It looks like I've let loose an epileptic dog in the back seat. So many holes to count, and so I do. Seventy-five days since the plane went down. Not even the whole season of spring. There is probably still ice on a river somewhere.

A noise at the window startles me. I drop the screwdriver. It rolls under the car floor mat. No one is there when I turn to the window, but it's early. Not many have ventured out yet and stretched themselves out to the sun. Some stretch like sunflowers or turtles. But they kid themselves. We are like neither of those things. We're not lucky enough to be firmly rooted in one place.

I crank the window down and crane my neck to look outside. The sun feels warm despite my breath being visibly carried away like a blanket of frost. Somewhere, a whine. Ever so faint. I look down and sigh. Brown's dog.

On the loose again. Always straying. Brown, I mean. Not the dog. Whenever Brown disappears, Shy comes to the bottom of my window. She looks like a vertically challenged car-hop, gazing at me, grinning her floppy dog smile, full of love and well-wishing.

"Shy," I call to her. She stretches her body up to meet me. She meekly licks the tips of my outstretched fingers.

"Where's your buddy?" I ask.

And then the noise starts. It's grating and discordant, ringing through the air. Low and guttural. The brutal, screaming sound of a moving metal octopus. I cringe and hold back a scream.

*It could be me this time*, I think.

*It could be me.*

The sound of tight whips and the snapping of cables assault my ears. Bending metal girders are giving out from the weight of the island and the ocean's abuse. The epitome of man's industrial creation is melting out from underneath us all, nothing more than a frail bar of sand. A whipping snap and a shriek of metal sends another one into the sea. I rest my chin on the sill of the warm window, as I watch it break off and disappear. It sinks noiselessly, without either regret or resolution.

No splash means no bodies. That time anyway. No

cries. It's a nice change. My eyes wander toward the bus. Toward *Elysium*.

They must have seen it go down. There are no worries for the folks on the bus. It's the unsinkable ship. It will never go down. And those on board – the Floaters – as we like to call them, they will never go down either. They will stay inside. Secure and comfortable, for as long as they can. But I'm sure they look out the window…

"No!" I hear a scream. "NOOOOOO!" Hoarse and defiant. Shy perks up immediately and out comes her tongue again.

Brown appears out of nowhere. He stops in front of my car hood and stares in horror at the gaping hole that had only moments before held a once bright and shiny 1955 red Plymouth. Fancy tail lights, fins and all. It still had a working radio that glowed a mellow green in the dark.

"We lost another one?" he shouts, as if questioning the higher powers. He snatches his hat off his head, wrings it with both hands and then slams it down on the car. He leans forward on the hood, balancing on his knuckles and hunched like a somnambulant ape, defeated. From my seat I can feel the impressive weight of his solid body.

"Shit!" he cries. "Shit… shit… shit…"

I honk my horn – more of a peep than a sincere honk. Just enough to stop him from steaming full ahead into a string of awful profanity. He lowers his gaze and observes me through the window. Chest heaving. Eyes starving. Angry.

"Shit," he concludes.

"It's a shitty world," I deduce, speaking through an open crack at the top of the passenger window, "but be yourself while you're in it. Cut out all that swearing. You don't have to impress me." I roll up the window.

I see him sigh, but straighten. He makes his way slowly over to the passenger side window and taps on the glass. I lean over and crank it down a bit.

"Can I come in," he asks, "and cool off?"

I gently pull up the lock fob which allows him to open the heavy door into my life. The weight of the car shifts uncomfortably as he eases himself beside me. He shuts the door and looks straight ahead at what lies before us. I am certain that he is watching *Elysium*, but he says nothing.

We sit for a minute. Shy trails off. Somewhere shady. Maybe into one of the other abandoned cars. She takes a gamble every time she climbs into one. We all do. Every wayward bump or nudge could easily upset something and submerge us all. Brown could be here today. And maybe gone the next. Nothing on this island of garbage is certain. No matter what we - the Drifters - want to believe.

Anyway, it doesn't matter too much what we believe any more now that there are so few of us left. Brown is the only Drifter I have seen for several mornings. I am beginning to think that we are the only ones left. But there are lots of hiding places on our island. Even with the constant threat of parts of the island sinking, there are still plenty of cars to hold us together.

"Cool now?" I ask. Stillness breaks between us. He nods.

"I'm sorry," I whisper. "About the car."

Brown smiles through tight lips. His name is not really Brown. I only call him that because of his beautiful skin which manages to look golden even on cloudy days. His real name is Bernhardt, though for some reason he insists on being called Bernie. I just call him Brown and he has never protested.

"I know she meant a lot to you. They all mean a lot."

He nods gently, and looks out at the bus which sports a line of tinted windows. We hear music wafting from its slightly open door. Shy reappears, slinking out of a nearby hollow of trash.

"If even one more comes loose, I am positive that we are going to sink," he says. He tries to rein in his light drawl for my benefit. His kind is not very good at picking up language dialects. He wasn't made for the use of his mouth. It was only his hands that were deemed useful back on the mainland.

He points to the bus. "Have you tried to get on it yet?" he asks. I shake my head.

"Why not?"

"For the same reason you don't. I belong out here. I will never be a Floater, Brown. I haven't been out of this car since we got here and it's been almost three months now."

He reclined back in his seat. "Is that all it's been? Three months!"

"Seventy-six days since the plane went down," I

reply. "Seventy-six days of watching you harness and rope together, mountains of trash. Watching you work miracles out of miles of auto wreckage, oil drums and jumper cables. I reach over and correct a fallen strand of his dark hair. "It feels like years, but it's only been three months."

Brown closes his eyes and pretends to feel my fingers loop his hair behind his ear.

"Anybody else out there with you this morning?" I ask.

"I was actually coming to see if you had Castor and Shane with you," Brown confessed. "Have you seen them today?"

"No, not today."

"What about Ira?"

I shake my head. "No, Brown. You and Shy have been the only ones. The others might still be asleep."

"It's late to be sleeping anywhere on the island. You sleep in the sun, next thing you know, you get a face full of hot metal."

"Some of the Drifters think that the Floaters have air-conditioning on their bus," I muse.

"I don't even want to know where they would get all of the energy to waste it like that." Brown's eyes open. "I have a pretty good idea though. I do. But I don't want to think about shit like that. I don't want to think about all the awful things that beings are capable of doing to each other."

My reticence turns his gaze toward the back seat. "What's the deal with all of those pock-marks in your upholstery?"

"They're keeping track of the days since the plane went down. Weren't you just listening to me?"

He runs his tapered fingers over the rips in the seat and feels my account of time slipping through his hands. "I think you're the only one keeping tabs on that around here. I think everyone else has given up."

"You haven't."

"I know", he looks at me, a smile playing around the corners of his mouth, "but in case you haven't noticed, I thrive in the company of disaster."

I smile. It's hard not to when I look at Brown's face. It emboldens him.

"It takes a very special person around here to get things done. While you are living in your car, feeling sorry for yourself and destroying your leather seats, I'm out keeping things afloat – no pun intended. With fewer people out here, and more people in there…" he points to the bus, "I'm a sheriff running a ghost town built on a pool of quicksand."

"Do you think that's where they all went?" I ask. "The other Drifters?"

"Sure," he says. "Where else do you think they would go?"

"You don't think that they just kind of floated away?"

"Well, not in the way you would think."

"Some of them could have been in that Plymouth…"

"They're all on *Elysium* now," Brown says with certainty. "They'd choose the bus before they'd suffocate in the tar sands."

"Well…"

"Look around you - the oil stretches out for miles. You'd never be able to swim far enough to clear it, and even if you did, where would you go? You want to go out that way?"

I say nothing.

"No!" he answers for me. "You wouldn't. Nobody in their right mind -"

"You would," I reply, and he smirks in a knowing way.

"Before I would take my chances with the Floaters? You bet I would. We, Drifters… I… I made this city. I knew when I roped it together with my bare hands that I intended to go down with my ship."

"I know."

"I'm not going to beg to hop aboard a bus filled with a bunch of delusional assholes who view the world they're doomed to through tinted glass. Our work keeps that sorry bunch on the bus alive. I'm not about to succumb to their politics."

I rest my chin on the window and close my eyes. The sun is hot now and the wind carries the rancid sweetness of midday.

Brown adds, "They only want us on the bus to get rid of us anyway."

"What do you mean?" I ask.

"Come on," Brown says. A faint chirp of a cynical laugh. "What about those screams you hear at night? They aren't shrieks of delight. You can't tell me that you don't see what goes on down at the Pit after dark."

"That's enough," I say. But Brown goes on. His

kind wasn't made to read the room.

"You're worse off than I thought, I guess – sitting in your car with blinders on and making a mess of your back seat."

The Pit is what we call the big, black eye of oily water languishing in the center of our dissolving island home. The precarious structure which we inhabit is shaped like a big metal donut. It is nervously strung together with tons of discarded rubber, abandoned cars, junkyard scraps and cubes of metal and forms a messy ring somewhere in the Pacific Ocean. The Black Oasis is just a romantic name for the largest unmitigated oil spill in the history of the world. It hovers in a congealed, globby mass, several miles from the New York coastline and covers one of earth's largest oceans for miles and miles. It's impossible to even guess how big it is.

From my window, I can't see where the blue of the ocean meets the sky. I can only see the tips of the Manhattan skyline in the far-off distance. It looks like an array of tiny nibs springing from an uncontrolled pool of black fountain ink. At night, we can see the lights of the city.

But on this ring, there is also a city. And the Black Oasis is divided between the Drifters and the Floaters. We divided out of fear. And for the sake of dividing. Two camps hopelessly set apart on this tiny piece of dead life that keeps us together. We may have defined our roles, but the island and its discord unite us all.

Forced into exile, we have all been set adrift on the Black Oasis to reflect upon our punishment for treason. There is a law against our very existence, and for this we are sentenced here to wait out our demise. It's death by island paradise.

"I'm pretty good at keeping my windows rolled up," I say. I have nothing more to add. I know. Everything he says is true.

Over one hundred and twenty of us were set adrift on a junk island less than an acre square. Tugboats pulled us and our new island home out into the mire, unhooked us and then departed. They pulled us out farther than I thought I would ever see of the water. Progress slowed measurably the further out we went. Our movements began to feel congealed, like we were sailing through a spill of cold molasses. The remainder of man's remedy to speed up the world was slowing us down to a painful crawl. The journey left us all ample time to contemplate our fate. We weren't segregated then. We huddled close and clustered together like a giant cult of blind lemmings, united in our horror.

Then it began to rain. And we were animals without an ark. Drops pelted down in a greasy, acidic fury like a shower of stones. The thick air pollution made being caught out in a rain storm equivalent to being ensnared in a torrential downpour of bird shit. It was considered more dangerous than a hurricane or typhoon. Rain was not pretty, or romantic or life-giving. Rain was lethal.

Screaming. Bodies running blindly. Falling. Slipping off the edge. Going in, down and under. Forgotten. Forever. I was caught up in a roving, hysterical crowd, the force of which knocked me to the ground. I prayed not to die that way. My body filling and then bursting open with the swell of humanity's thick, black sickness.

I prayed not to be trampled. And as I prayed, I first noticed the bus. Or actually, I noticed the number of us who were now beginning to swarm toward the bus in a great desperate migration. The maroon colored machine stuck out like a Holy beacon rising up from the middle of the decay. The front half of the door was visible, hanging open like a broken jaw. On the side, in red and yellow cursive, it read: *Elysium Tours*. And the crowd was driven to it. They charged and clamored over each other in the midst of the acid torrent. Bodies leapt into the open door and clung to the bus's side, helplessly, like so many lolling tongues.

Others less fortunate hung onto the disintegrating seams of the island. Open eyes sizzled and bubbled like frying eggs in the relentless downpour. On the mainland, there were shelters and procedures for disastrous nature like this. Alarms would warn us that rain was coming. We had a chance there, and most of us who were suffering here would have had protection on the mainland. But there was no protection here. Out of desperation, I joined the fray.

The rain didn't stop the stoic tugboats. They kept dragging us further out. They may have been whistling out of their smokestacks with delight. And I crawled through the twisting and burning rubble on my hands and knees, keeping time with their song. Clamoring feet pounded at me. All around me the desperate sounds of the fight for survival. Bodies wrenched from the precarious edges went over the sides.

But they weren't splashing.

They were *splooshing*.

A horrid thickly wet and disgusting sound. So unspeakable and final.

*If I can just make it to the bus,* I thought.

*To Elysium*

I began to slip off the edge of the island when suddenly a hand grabbed my belt loop and yanked me back from the burning sludge. I went limp and felt weightless. I was pulled back from the swirling well which was becoming the wet center eye. The rain was creating a roiling, black hole that threatened to suck us all in.

Bodies raced past me. One after the other taking each other's places in the mindless herd. A young boy fell near me. He was pushed to his knees and tipped backwards over the edge into the eye of the Oasis. The act occurred with so much macabre grace that it could have passed for synchronized swimming.

A bellow amidst the chaos: "On your feet!"

The hand tugged at me, helping me find grounding. Then a big arm wrapped around me. It cloaked my vision and my face pressed into the crook of a shoulder that smelled like kerosene.

We started moving, and I felt so light. More *splooshing* sounds of burning bodies being lost on the hopeless journey to *Elysium*. And then we stop. I hear a great solid *click*. The opening of an old car door – heavy and firm. It is the sound of something that was built to last forever. Without warning, I am flung into exactly what I imagined. I fall on to something soft and warm and immediately try to weep.

The door slams shut, and all at once the frantic world is muffled. Outside seems distant. Elsewhere. And this discarded car is now my world. I'm crumpled in the front driver's seat. A thin veil of steel and glass separates me from the horrors of the panic and insanity that I so narrowly escaped. I hear their cries and moans.

A dog barks! A dog was exiled? Even a dog nowadays is prone to piss off the reigning anarchy.

The closing of the door behind him presses Kerosene Man firmly up against me. We are neck-in-neck and face-to-face. My sobs meet his stoic silence. He stares at me as though we have known each other all of our lives.

He's a big man with a thick neck, but shockingly delicate features. Brooding black hair and eyes. Red streaks from the acid rain line his face clearly, like lace patterns on a doily. It is already starting to eat through his clothes, but he is all right. He's wearing coveralls. He has a name tag: BERNIE.

Bernie takes the back of my head in his hands and presses my forehead to his. And we shut our eyes to each other like lovers about to kiss. Outside, the brutalized masses scream loudly and Bernie whispers gently in my ear.

"Baseball," he whispers. "I loved baseball on Sundays. I'd watch it on the color t.v., but I was close enough to the stadium to watch it in person if I climbed the tree on the edge of the parking lot."

Great groans of metal and the sweet smell of sulfur.

"I never watched baseball," I whisper back.

"You missed out," he smiles. Behind us, a body

slams against the back window and someone begins to scream uncontrollably.

And I never leave the car again.

I only started keeping track of the days after the plane went down. That was the real holocaust of the Black Oasis. That was the day we lost most of the island's Drifter population to blind hope.

A few days after we had been on the Oasis, I awoke one morning to a high-pitched whine. It was the sound of a great machine in distress. Near the island's perimeter, the engines of a downed Boeing jet airliner plane were sputtering about in the goo as it slowly submerged. One of the engines overloaded, and then exploded, sending shards of grey shrapnel and streaks of smoky flame into the sky.

I watched the engine roil and as the mushroom cloud formed in the sky and danced around the sparks and flames, floating in perfect harmony with the music of its exhausted fans, I watched for Bernie. Bernie, unlike me, made a daily habit of leaving the safety of the car, and being out with the others, looking for hopeful solutions to the island's insurmountable problems. His hope had taken him that day to a place out of my sight.

I had fireflies in my stomach and a hand tightly clenched around one of the door handles. A part of me wanted to run. Run to find Bernie and bring him back. And another part of me wanted to run. Run right into the blissful, blazing energy of that beautiful damned machine.

And then I saw him running toward the car. His

hand reached for the latch. His black eyes were riveted towards the source of danger and desire. I popped the lock fob. He jerked the handle open and slid into the seat beside me, closing the door with a thump behind him.

That's when we noticed the others begin jumping into the ocean like lemmings. Drawn to the energy of the engine, they disappeared into the smoking abyss which they foolishly mistook as their ticket to heaven.

Amidst the throngs of the frantic crowd, *Elysium* rocked and its door came ajar. We both waited for a barrage of Floaters to join the fray, but not a single one of them left the bus. The remaining engine of the sinking plane wailed and screamed, churning its way through the thick poison.

I could feel the whole fragile island rocking beneath the car. Out of nowhere a man leapt onto the hood. More Drifters followed. The commotion of frantic feet climbing over us punched dents into the car roof. The last engine finally exploded, bursting into a ball of fire and incinerating all who managed to brave the Pit and swim out to meet this brewing vat of malignant energy. They were incinerated. Moths to a flame.

Brown later said that it had to have been over fifty Drifters that fought their way towards that sinking ball of energy.

And when the Boeing had finally disappeared beneath the heavy oil slick and into the salty ocean brine below, Brown cupped my head in his hands and kissed my forehead in an awful, gentle way. I began to count the days that I lived through after that, as though I needed constant reassurance that our world could, at any moment, crumble underneath us, and vanish entirely.

But Brown doesn't keep track of the days like I do. He finds it a pointless exercise. He would rather keep track of the inventory of the immediate world around us. In the morning when I wake up, he's already up and moving stealthily, making mental notes on the berg which now sustains us and wondering how he can make it last longer than it is supposed to. He's a born fixer, a preserver and a fighter. I wonder how he keeps his hope alive that we are going to make it through. He believes that we can go on living here forever, and I just can't bring myself to contradict this vibrant hope. It is not my place to share my despair.

He comes to see me after his rounds each morning, when the light is strong enough and the sun high enough to crack through the polluted grey sky. This morning, he's been out counting cars. He tallies the ones that we've lost and the ones that are still hanging on. He tries to take a tally of the Drifters who have gone down like the cars. Who has broken off? Who has miraculously held on? Who has managed to avoid the temptation of begging for shelter on the bus? Who has escaped the temptation of the Pit?

"It's not fair that Shy is here with me," he turns to me one hot afternoon as we sit together in the front seat watching the tour bus for activity.

"It's not fair that you let them send her," I respond.

"They would have stripped her otherwise. I couldn't face that thought," Brown says. "If anyone is going to strip my dog, it's going to be me. And I'll say when it needs to be done. They can't take that away from me."

"Wouldn't it have been better just to let her life end right there?" I ask.

"Not for me."

"So, you admit it then. Don't go blaming everyone else for your own weakness or inability to make a decision. If she suffers here, it's your fault." I turn away from him and hunch over the steering wheel.

"You've got to stop feeling sorry for yourself," Brown says after a moment. "Or before you know it, you won't be able to stand another day. Anyway," he says dismissively, "soon you'll be out of the car and on to that bus. No more scratches in the upholstery," he says quietly. "And then I'll be alone."

"You'd have your dog with you," I remind him.

"You're not getting the point, Io!" he barks.

"You're wrong!" I snap back. "I get the point. I get all of it!"

"There's not enough life on this berg to sustain us," Brown tries to cry but no tears fall. "Pretty soon, I'll have to strip her, whether I want to or not and then there will be just the two of us."

He smacks his old hat on the dashboard, startling me.

"And even if we share her, there wouldn't be enough," he screams. "That car, dammit! That car! I tied it up, Io! I did! It shouldn't have come loose that easily. It still had life in it. Still had life," his voice trails off softly.

"The radio even glowed. It glowed green as grass while it played. Did you see it?"

"I saw it," I say, keeping my gaze fixed on the tour bus. "But there's still this one," I reach out my thumb to jab at the power button. The radio surges to life and warbles into the silence of the afternoon.

"Turn it off," Brown says and punches the same button with his big finger. "Save it. I don't feel tired yet."

"I'm just saying this car has a good battery. It still has life. It's still pretty strong. Come here at night and you'll be safe from the outside. I'm sure that this car still has enough energy for both of us to live on for a while."

"Really?" he asks. I nod.

"I can bring provisions," he offers, as though he feels that he has to barter for his keep. "I've found a few things. Things still with life. I'll bring them over later. We can put them in the back seat and surround ourselves with them. We'll be safe."

"Okay," I manage to smile – a trifle intrigued. For the first time in months, a small trickle of hope rushes through me.

He moves to get out. Shy is resting on the hood of the car, facing the sun and the hazy, smelly wind, in a valiant pose.

"I'll be right back," Brown promises.

"Don't be promising things," I call after him. "You never know when you might…wind down."

"Like the airplane?" he asks, and then slams the door. He tromps off into the unknown like a soldier. Shy doesn't follow. She knows that there is likely more energy under the hood of the car than what Brown will bring back. I close my eyes and try to imagine what it would be like to watch a baseball game from a high tree. Brown returns when the day is at its hottest, carrying a raggedy mottle of electrical odds and ends. He dumps it all out into the back seat before collapsing from near exhaustion beside me.

"I think we're good," he pants.

"I'm turning on the radio," I say. I don't like the way he looks. His skin is very red.

"No," he stutters angrily and swats my hand away from the dashboard. "I don't need it."

"Sure…" I answer uncertainly. I take a moment to glance at his findings. He's brought a frayed octopus outlet fringed with the ends of old extension cords. The lower jaw of a broken Panini press with no cord. A "Hello Kitty" electric toothbrush with the ensign: "I LOVE NY" scrawled across the body. A potato clock with no connecting wire. A bubble gum penny bank. A children's book with an interactive electronic voice and touch pad buttons. A computer mouse. A string of Christmas lights. Crayons. And an "ETCH-A-SKETCH."

"Look," he says and reaches for the toothbrush. He sticks the bristle end in my unsuspecting mouth and flips the switch. The small muffled buzz of movement feels like a shooting star of orchestral glory. Suddenly, I am overcome with the emotion of loving joy. I immediately feel inexplicable glee and energy. My eyes become brighter. I feel alive.

"Now you," I say, and grab the brush so I can do the same for him. He shakes his head, instead whistling sharply. Shy jumps up to the driver's window and regards us calmly.

"Where's her chip?" I ask.

"In her ear," he replies, and so it is there that I position the bristles of the toothbrush. I flip the switch and "I LOVE NY" whirs to life. Within a moment, Shy's coat becomes glossier and smoother. She yips and pants. She is all the things that a happy dog in the prime of her life should be. After shoving the buzzing brush into Brown's reluctant mouth, we both collapse into a state of relaxed euphoria, sinking into each other's arms with a contented smile.

"Brown," I finally ask. "What kept you away?"

"You mean," he asks, "from the plane?"

"Yeah," I say. I don't have to explain anything to him. It's marvelous.

"I think it was because I heard the car radio playing," he muses.

"The radio was playing," I repeat softly.

"Don't you remember?" he asks. "It was an old, weird tune, and it was enough for me to stay."

"A measly car radio?" I ask in disbelief.

"Sometimes that's all you need," Brown closes his eyes and smiles back.

"But it was a PLANE!" I say. "A jumbo jet with the power to soar over countries, oceans, the WORLD! Didn't you, just for a moment, want to be part of that energy?"

"That's the reason why so many raced to it," he agreed. "After all, who doesn't want to have the power of Superman? Right? Faster than a speeding bullet.

More powerful than a fighter jet."

"Locomotive," I correct.

"Gesundheit," he winks. "That's the reason that there are so few of us left. We are so desperate that we can't resist. Think about it rationally, Io. None of us could withstand or harness the power of a jet plane."

"Do you think," I venture, "that they thought: *If I could just get close enough…?*"

"Sure," Brown affirms casually. "I think that some people will try anything to escape their fate. The mess they created. What they are afraid to face. People will try to escape anything that they fear. I think that's why we were dragged out here – us and thousands more we don't even know about – with the rest of their trash. People never want to face the unhappy consequences of what they themselves have created. They are happier to live in denial. To just put it behind them - an out of sight, out of mind situation. But one day, they will have so much put behind them that it will just swallow them all, cave in on them and they won't even know what hit them. I don't know what will finally be the straw that breaks it, but I do know that it's not us that humans should fear."

"Well, we don't need to fear humans anymore, at least," I say.

"No," Brown's voice lowers. "Now we have to contend with ourselves," he whispers. "And what we have become."

"I'll bet, if you put all of us together, we'd have the power of a fighter jet," I muse as I look out towards *Elysium*, which lights up each evening with the oncoming darkness. When darkness falls, light is plentiful in the land of the Floaters.

"I bet you're right," Brown says, joining me in my surveillance now. His mind is occupied. His voice is low, slow, monotonous, as though he has just switched on to auto pilot.

"We could sustain them for years, if they stretch us out..." he says.

Not far beyond, a light begins to glow brightly and life begins behind the tinted windows of the tour bus.

"...If they ration us out and strip us down thoroughly, one at a time."

We sit in silence as the darkness envelopes the car. We refrain from playing the radio.

The next morning, while Brown's eyes are still closed, I pull out the tiny screwdriver. I lean over into the back seat and tear another hole in the pocked upholstery.

Last night, we were surprised to see that no Floaters left the bus for demonstrations. All they did was light up the bus. We both wondered why. Neither of us wanted to express our optimism, but it was in our thoughts all the same.

"They're saving themselves up," Brown muses. "Usually they would demonstrate if they had something to burn, but their energy supplies must be getting scarce."

I shift uneasily in my seat as I witness their light fading with the coming dawn.

"It looks like they might be running out of energy," Brown says.

"What does that mean for us?" I ask.

"It means that we sit tight and don't make any noise. It means they might be too weak to get off the bus and search for more of us. It means they might just stay there and burn themselves out. If we're lucky, they'll think that all of the Drifters that haven't boarded the bus already have burned themselves out."

"Maybe..." I say to him and reach for the scrubby penny bank. I start turning the crank over and over and over. The clicking noise soothes me. "I hope we're not gone by then."

"Well, I'm not going to be Floater fuel," he swears and swipes the empty penny bank from my hands, the clank of a few stray pennies still rattling inside.

"Stop that!" he says. "You're making me nervous."

"Then hand me that book," I say and point to his mound of garbage in the back seat.

"Humans taught you how to read?" Brown asks.

"No," I shake my head. "I can only pretend. But the words are not the point."

He reaches over the seat and grabs the book, handing it to me. I open the flap and we begin to lose ourselves in the colorful pictures. There is an image of a boy with a baseball glove falling from an apple tree. Brown once again tries to cry.

On day eighty-one, Shy goes missing. Brown finds her in her favorite shady spot – an old icebox – but this time with the door closed tight shut. She is lying in the bottom of the ice box with a serene expression on her foxy little face. Her legs are crossed in front of her, like a lady's. Between her paws is the "Hello Kitty" electric toothbrush. Both she and the brush are dead.

Brown brings her back to the car and slides her body into the seat behind me. He flings the toothbrush out of the window as he settles into his own seat.

"She took the brush," is all he says. His eyes are defeated; glazed over with a kind of hopelessness. But there is no remorse in his face. No remorse at finding her all wound down, like an old pocket-watch. Remorse is for humans. Which we are not. In the situations where humans find travesties, we always seem to find efficiencies.

"She kept out of the sun," Brown says finally. "She'll last a while."

And she does. We carefully dismantle her body and press ourselves against her mechanical insides, absorbing every last bit of energy in her artificial husk.

It takes four days to share her. And as we struggle to maintain ourselves, we also constantly monitor the Floaters. There hasn't been any sign of life on *Elysium* for nearly a week and there is no end to how nervous that makes us feel. We sit in silence for long stretches at a time, watching the bus, as day turns to night and back again.

"Are they done, do you think?" I finally ask Brown.

He doesn't respond, but seems to be wondering the same thing. In his hands he holds the remains of the crayons. He chews on them endlessly, as though they are a vital energy resource. But it's only like chewing gum – it's filling an empty, habitual need that gets him nowhere. He's on his very last color which is powder blue.

"I'm burning her remains," Brown suddenly says.

"What?" I ask. "What are you going on about?"

"We need to burn her," he reasons. "Like the humans do to the ones they love. We can burn her in the Pit."

"We're *not* human," I am incensed, but careful not to shout. "You're being irrational. If we go out and burn her body in the Pit, the Floaters will see us for sure."

"I don't want to die knowing that we made her stay on this island. She's a piece of my life that I don't want to just discard her like trash!" Brown voices passionately.

"You are *not* human. How can you discard a piece of your life if you, yourself, are not a living thing?" I ask in exasperation.

He turns to me, seething with an anger that I had never before seen in him, or thought could be real in someone like us.

"Would you stop trying to sound as though you have a clue as to what those words mean!" he almost screams.

I don't break my gaze, but I also do not respond. Because I know what he's saying is true. I really shouldn't have any idea what these words really mean. Especially what they mean to him. But I'm frozen, because at this moment, I do. I think really I do.

"I may not be living, but I am *not* something that the world can just so easily use up and – and – *THROW AWAY*," he shouts.

Brown scrambles out of his seat, slaps his hat on his head, and gathers up the remains of his dog.

"You've given up," he states flatly as he eases Shy's remains out of the back seat of the car. "You think that this is where we are meant to end up, but you're wrong! This is only the place where humans think we should be. But *Elysium* isn't home and this junk island isn't home, and this isn't the end for us! I am not a part of this scrap heap. Neither is Shy!"

He looks at me with pitiful contempt.

"And neither are you."

He slams the car door and I watch him walk away.

"Brown!" I scream. I couldn't care less now whether the Floaters hear me or not. I only want him to come back. "Brown, don't be stupid! Stupidity is for *HUMANS!*"

But he keeps walking anyway, towards the center of the Black Oasis. To the Pit. To the well of oil and acid rain and muck. Brown becomes a silhouette in the orange glow of the setting sun. Shy's parts bob up and down as they hang limply from his arms. And for a moment, he is walking with such purpose and stalwart virtue and mercy that you could almost mistake him for a living being; one with all human flaws and compassion, one with eyes that can shed salty tears, and with a beating heart that can feel pain, and that wrenches and breaks.

I look around desperately, suspended in horror amidst the cavalcade of broken electronic waste and slashes in the red upholstery. All this energy conserving and rational time-tracking – all just a pointless exercise of selfish routine now that I am alone. I watch Brown stop at the Pit's shore. He bends down and ceremoniously lays the parts of Shy in front of him as if he were placing a gathering of flowers at a crypt. He is so gentle with her that I can hardly bear to watch.

I desperately want to join him in his ceremony but fear drives me to remain a spectator. I am overwhelmed with the need to share his sorrow or his attempt to feel sorrow. But I cannot leave the car. I have not left the car in such a long time. And Brown has always come back. But something tells me that Brown is not coming back to the car this time. And then, the screech of metal pierces the dusky air and I snap my gaze toward the bus. Towards *Elysium*. Floaters!

"Brown!" I scream again. "Brown! Floaters! Floaters! *FLOATERS!*"

But he won't hear me. He's trying to spark a flame by scraping together the remains of two metal shards. A shower of sparks fly into the air only to die quickly in the evening breeze. He bends down further to rest on his knees, getting closer to the oily waste. Sparks fly once more.

Floaters are painstakingly descending from the bus cabin steps. I watch with horror as their condition becomes clear. Most of them are missing their vital parts. Many of them have strips of skin flayed away from their frames. It nakedly reveals their wire and metal construction. Many of the wrecks shambling from *Elysium* can't even walk upright. But all are determined to reach Brown and the energy that he is emitting. I realize with certainty that their missing parts have been sacrificed for their own energy consumption. It occurs to me suddenly that perhaps it was not the Drifters camp that had suffered the most. While we envied what the Floaters had inside of *Elysium,* they really had nothing more than we did. The emaciated pack of Floaters looks as though they are ready to wind down and wink out of existence. To become part of the Black Oasis that holds us all captive.

Brown pretends not to notice the potential danger. He strikes the scraps of metal once more, this time very close to the water. All at once, flames engulf Shy and the oily water in which she rests. Brown stands up, takes his baseball cap off his head and holds it over his chest.

"Oooooohhhhhh, say… Can you … Seeeeee?" he belts out.

The Floaters come closer, uninhibited by the rising blue flames which seem to be swallowing Brown from the ground up.

"Byyy the Daunterlyyyyy… Liiiiiiiggghhtttt…What so prrrroudly…"

The flames rise higher as the wasted and destroyed mechanical creations come nearer to Brown. They seem undeterred by the menace of the incinerating oil-fed heat. Brown's pulsing energy feels tremendous. I can feel it from all the way in my car. It brightens me. I feel even brighter than the day that Brown shoved the toothbrush into my mouth and turned it on. It makes me feel as though I am surrounded by some impenetrable force: a force that protects me. His light allows me to transcend my fear. I feel as though I can do anything.

And suddenly, I cannot find my tiny screwdriver fast enough. I am on a mad hunt for it, and it takes me a moment in my glorious ecstasy to remember that I rested it behind my ear, like a human would do with a pen or a pencil. I yank it from its hiding place and plunge it into the ignition, like a kid trying to unlock a closed door with a hair pin.

"And the rocket's red flaaaarrrrrrrrrrrrrre...!"

"Come on," I whisper. "Come on. *Come on.*"

"The bombs bursting in aaaaaiiiiiiiiiiiiiirrrrrrrrrrrr!"

And then a great, swampy growl engulfs me and the massive car that has been both my home and my prison surges to life. The dashboard lights come alive in all of their green glory. The headlights cut through the oncoming gloom. There's still life in us both. This is a certainty now.

I punch my foot down into the dark abyss underneath, searching for the gas pedal. I pump it and the car roars with a ravenous, gurgling appetite.

The Floaters crane their necks towards me, and the car headlights blind them. They stop, frozen solid in their wobbly tracks.

"Keep singing!" I shout to Brown, who has now turned to see the great commotion. The flames are dancing at his waist – even a little higher.

"Came throoooooouuuuuuughhhhhhhhhhh...in the NIIIIIIIIGGGGGGHHHHTTTTTTT!" he wails.

I pop the clutch and the car lurches forward, fighting against all of the compacted trash that has held it for so long. The Floaters have now turned their entire attention to me and the car, but I am no longer afraid. There is so much light surrounding me that I feel immortal. I could go on forever.

"Buuuuuuuuut our flaaggggggggggg was stillllllllll

theerrrrrrrrrrrrre…" Brown's voice carries over the engine's noise.

It is difficult driving over the hurdles of junk. The flattened tires squeal and complain. The rusted holes in the floorboards let the sludgy water in. This island made from human refuse is very thinly constructed. At any moment, we could all be lost to its spontaneous dismemberment. But I am no longer afraid of surprise endings. There is no one infringing on the ending that I am about to write for my existence. There is only Brown and me, and the sound of Brown's tuneless song.

Floaters are tripping over each other and the heaps of trash to get at me and my car. Some are falling through the gaping cracks in the island, disappearing into the water. Some are caught in the flames of Shy's funeral pyre. Some are clawing at the car to get in, but I steam forward, lurching onward toward the Pit where Brown now stands, singing his heart out.

The car reaches the edge of the Pit's shore and rests precariously, rocking back and forth.

"Forrrrrrr the laaaaaaaaaaaand of the freeeeeeeeeeeee!" Brown screams.

"Get in, Brown!" I honk the horn robustly. It sounds like bells ringing out on a Sunday morning. Calling us to where we need to go.

Brown drags himself over to the passenger door and reaches up for the handle. I can see that he is burned away from the waist down. His coveralls are tattered remnants of a life long forgotten. His nametag – BERNIE – is nowhere to be found.

I lean over to pull his great body, which still has

amazing girth in his upper torso, into the front seat and close to me. He pulls the door tight behind him. What remains of him sparks and sizzles unceremoniously, but his face sports a wide smile.

"And the home of the brave," he sighs.

The struggle of pulling Brown into the car tips it, nose forward, and we begin to sink slowly. The angry and desperate screams of the Floaters surround us as they watch the last of the Drifters leave the Black Oasis in style. The last two Drifters which will not be used up only to be thoughtlessly discarded.

Their groans and wails can be heard over the entire island, but I don't much care for their song, so I decide to turn on the radio.

Casually, I ask Brown: "Wherever did you learn to sing a song like that?"

He smiles softly in the mellow green glow of the dashboard lights.

"Baseball players used to sing it before they played their games. Even if they were playing away from home, they sang it. I think it was to remind themselves that wherever they were, they still belonged somewhere."

"And here we go with the wind up – and the pitch," the radio announces smoothly. "And there's the play at the plate! Safe at second, folks! And, Holy Cow! Safe at third! Turn on the juice! Let's see if he makes it home!"